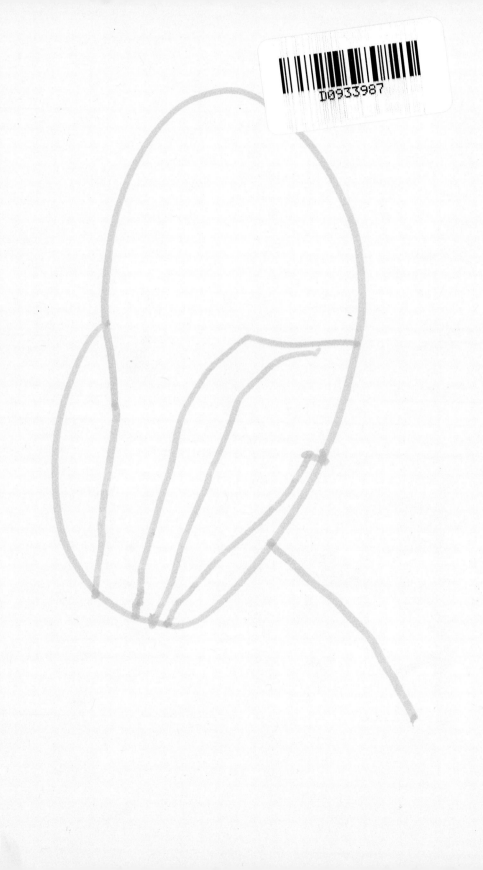

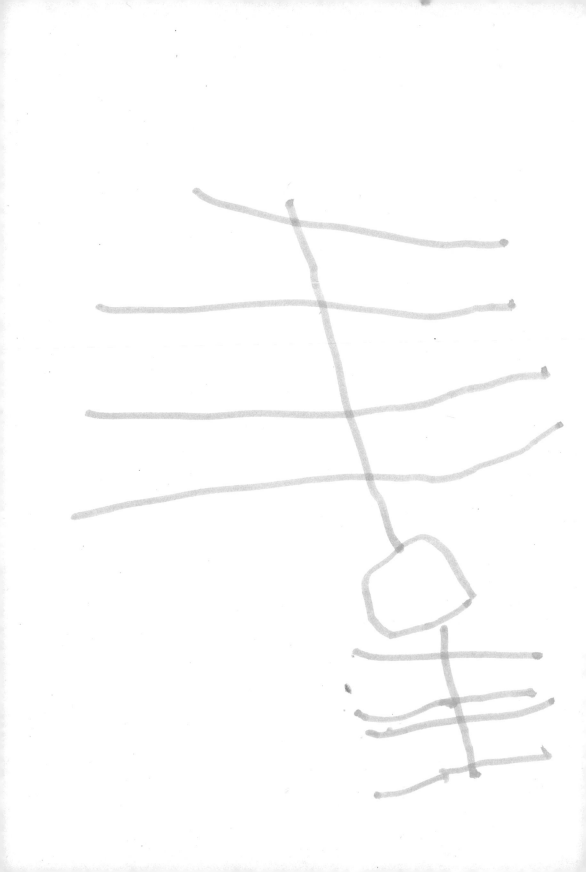

Tiggy and the
giant wave

Grolier Enterprises Inc. offers a varied selection of both
adult and children's book racks. For details on ordering,
please write: Grolier Enterprises Inc., Sherman Turnpike,
Danbury, CT 06816 Attn: Premium Department

Published in the United States by Grolier Enterprises, Inc.
Danbury, Connecticut 06816.

Originally published in the United States by
Modern Promotions/Publishers, a Division of Unisystems, Inc.

Designed by Victoria House Publishing Limited, Paulton, Bristol BS18 5LQ.

Jane Carruth   illustrated by Tony Hutchings

Tiggy and the giant wave

GROLIER ENTERPRISES INC.
Danbury, Connecticut 06816

Tiggy was helping Mommy make strawberry jam when Daddy put his head around the door. "I've got news for you!" he cried. "Uncle Pintog has asked us to spend Saturday with him."
Tiggy knew that Uncle Pintog had once been a sailor and that he lived at the seashore.

Tiggy had never been to the seashore. "What is it like?" she kept asking Mommy. When Saturday came at last, Mommy gave her a surprise present, a brand new pail and shovel. "Can Teddy come to the shore with us?" Tiggy asked, as they were leaving. Mommy said that Teddy would have to stay behind and guard the house.

Daddy had borrowed Herbert Hare's old car to take them to the seashore. He made sure they were wearing their seat belts before he drove off.

"Tell me again about the ocean and the sand," Tiggy whispered to Mommy, as they drove along.

"Well," said Mommy, "the sand is a warm golden color, and the ocean is blue with little waves. Sometimes there are big waves."

It didn't seem very long before they were at the seashore. Standing there was Uncle Pintog, in a funny kind of shirt with stripes and a sea captain's cap, waving to them. "We mustn't waste a minute," he shouted in a jolly voice. "Let's go straight to the beach for a picnic."

Tiggy loved the warm, golden sand and soon Uncle Pintog
was helping her build a big sandcastle. ''Oh, the seashore is
fun!'' she cried. ''I could stay here for ever and ever.''
''It's fun splashing about in the ocean, too,'' said jolly Uncle
Pintog. ''Come on, Tiggy, what do you say? We'll go down
to the water together.''
''You go with Uncle Pintog,'' said Daddy, in a sleepy kind
of voice. ''He'll take care of you.''

Tiggy wasn't quite sure if she liked wading in the ocean. She kept tight hold of Uncle Pintog's hand as the little waves splashed over her feet. "Keep your dress out of the water," Uncle Pintog warned her, laughing. "Now, isn't this fun! You're not scared, are you?"

Then, all at once, a wave much bigger than the others came rushing towards Tiggy. Tiggy was so frightened by the giant wave that she tried to run away from it. The giant wave was too quick for her. It knocked her over and Tiggy began to cry.

Poor Tiggy! She could not stop crying—not even when
Mommy told her that Uncle Pintog and Daddy had gone to
find a big surprise for her. "I hate the ocean," Tiggy
sobbed, as Mommy rubbed her dry. "My dress is all wet.
I-I want to go home and see Teddy."
"What nonsense!" said Mommy. "That naughty wave was
just playing a game with you."

But Tiggy would not be comforted. "I-I won't ever go wading in the ocean again!" she sobbed.

While the warm sun was drying Tiggy's dress, she saw
Daddy and Uncle Pintog coming towards them carrying
something big and brightly colored.
"What is it?" Tiggy asked. "What can it be? I've never seen
anything like it before!"
"It's Uncle Pintog's surprise," said Mommy.

"Now then, Tiggy," cried Uncle Pintog in his loud sailor's voice. "I've brought you your own wading pool. Come on, help us fill it." But Tiggy would only watch while Uncle Pintog, his little friends, and Daddy began pouring water into the pool.

Tiggy soon grew tired of sitting with Mommy. "I think I will help," she said at last. Mommy smiled as Tiggy picked up her new pail and ran down to the water's edge.
"That's my brave girl," said Daddy. "With your help, we will soon fill the pool."

It wasn't long before Tiggy and Mommy were standing in Uncle Pintog's beautiful little pool.

"This is fun," Tiggy laughed. "And there are no giant waves to chase me!"

"Your uncle is full of surprises," said Mommy.

There were more surprises for Tiggy when, at the end of the day, they all went back to Uncle Pintog's strange little house for something to drink. His living room looked like the cabin of an old ship. There were big treasure chests and model ships and even an old anchor.

Tiggy could hardly drink her milk she was so busy looking around her. And then Uncle Pintog began telling wonderful stories of his adventures at sea. ''Ah, those were the days, Tiggy!'' he sighed. And Tiggy wondered if the treasure chests were filled with gold he had won from fierce pirates.

Afterwards, Tiggy helped Mommy take the cups and saucers into the kitchen while Daddy and Uncle Pintog put a large, mysterious package in the back of the car. Then it was time to go home. Tiggy was so busy waving to her jolly uncle and her new little friends that she didn't notice the strange package in the car.

What a surprise the next day when Tiggy found Uncle
Pintog's wading pool in the garden! "Uncle Pintog wanted
you to have it," said Daddy. "I brought it back in the car."
"I wonder if Teddy will like wading?" said Tiggy. "It's not
as good as the real ocean, but Uncle Pintog couldn't send
us the real waves and the real sand, could he?"
Daddy shook his head. "Perhaps Teddy will soon see the
ocean for himself," he smiled.

And after all, Tiggy didn't have long to wait to show Teddy the ocean, for the very next Saturday they were all back with Uncle Pintog. He seemed jollier than ever and soon he insisted Tiggy and Teddy join him in the water.

"You hold Teddy tightly," he told Tiggy. "And I'll hold you tightly."
Tiggy laughed. "Then if that giant wave does come along we'll be ready for it."